HI
NEW
BABY!

written by
Robie H. Harris

illustrated by
Michael Emberley

CANDLEWICK PRESS
CAMBRIDGE, MASSACHUSETTS

I'll never ever forget the moment you met your new baby brother. "Oh!" you said. "Oh!" is all you said. You didn't say anything else. But you did stare at the baby — for a very long time. Then the baby wiggled his nose, sneezed, and yawned. But he didn't wake up.

"That baby doesn't do anything!" you finally said. "That baby's so tiny. Its nose is so tiny. And it's still sleeping. I wish it would wake up!"

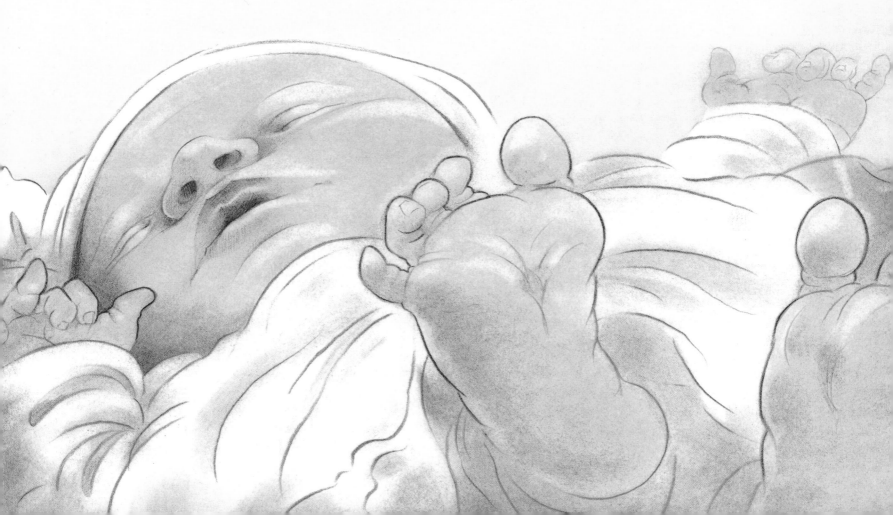

Then you touched the baby's nose with your finger. And he woke up, opened his mouth wide—and began to cry! And you covered your ears with your hands as fast as you could.

Mommy picked up the baby and
cuddled him tight.

"It's crying! It's too noisy!"
you said in a loud voice.
"Make it stop, Daddy!"

You quickly climbed onto my lap.
"I do not like that baby!" you whispered.

"But I bet he'll like having a big sister,"
I whispered back. And I gave you a hug
and a kiss.

I cuddled you, and you cuddled your
furry stuffed bear. I loved having you all
snug in my arms. You still fit in my lap.
But you certainly weren't a baby anymore.

Soon the new baby stopped crying
and fell asleep again.

"I've seen the baby," you whispered
to me. "So let's go home now!"
And we did.

The next morning, after you and I brought Mommy and the baby home, they took a nap. We ate a piece of Grandma's cake—our favorite— even though it was still morning.

"I was never as tiny as that new baby!" you said.

"You were that tiny," I told you, "but that was a long time ago."

"I don't remember when I was a baby," you said.

"Oh, you were the most WONDERFUL baby!" I said.

"But now you're a big kid," I told you. "Now you're our big kid."

"I'm not that big!" you shouted, as you grabbed your furry stuffed bear and hugged it tight. Then you gave your bear a kiss on its nose.

"I have a baby too," you said. "My bear is my baby. And my bear is way more fun than your baby!"

"I like your baby a lot!" I told you.

"I'm going to show Mommy my baby!" you said. And you ran off to show her.

"Here's my baby!" you told Mommy,
as you held up your furry stuffed bear.
"I like your furry baby!" she said.
"Do you like your baby?" you asked.
"We love the new baby," she said. "And we
love you! We always have and we always will!"
And then she gave you a hug and a kiss.
Then you looked at the new baby and
told Mommy, "Your baby's so-ooo
boring! I wish it would
DO something!"

Suddenly, the baby began to cry again. You muttered, "Crybaby!"

"The baby's hungry," I told you. "That's why he's crying."

"I'm hungry too!" you cried. You and I ate grilled cheese sandwiches with pickles in the middle. Mommy fed the new baby, and ate a pickle. Then the new baby spit up.

"That baby is icky!" you said. "I never spit up! And I can feed myself. That baby can't!"

Then you grabbed the new baby's hat off the kitchen table—and put the hat on your head. It sat on the tippy-tippy top! It fit! But it barely fit.

"See, Daddy," you shouted as you pointed to the hat. "Now I'm the baby!"

"See, Mommy!" you shouted, as you pointed to the hat again. "Now I'm the baby in this family! And one baby is enough!"

Later on, when Grandma and Grandpa came to visit,
the baby began to hiccup. Grandma held him
over her shoulder, and you patted the baby's back. The
baby burped. Then he drooled. Then he spit up again.
Then you watched Grandpa change the baby's diaper.
"That baby is yucky!" you said. "It pees in a diaper.
I pee in the toilet! That baby
can't!" you told me.

Then the baby looked at you—and yawned.

"That baby doesn't have any teeth!" you said. "I have so-ooo many teeth. And I can brush all my teeth. That baby can't!"

Then you smiled at the baby, opened your mouth wide, and showed him all your teeth. The baby opened his mouth wide too—just like you. But he began to cry.

"I don't cry all the time like that baby does!" you said.

"That's because YOU are a big sister," I told you.

"And he's only a little baby," you said.

You looked at the baby again. And then you said,
"I'm way bigger than he is!"

"You're even big enough to hold the baby," I told you.

"I am?" you asked.

"You sure are!" I said. "Big sisters are big!"

"Big sisters are too big to wear baby hats!"
you said. And you took the baby's hat
off your head—and slipped it
on the baby's head.

"Hi new baby!" you whispered. And the baby looked up at you—and stopped crying! I laid the baby in your lap, and you rocked him in your arms. You looked so big. He looked so little.

"YOU are the baby in this family!" you whispered to him. "And one baby is enough!" Then you gave him a kiss on his nose. Soon the baby fell fast asleep.

"I like the baby quiet," you whispered. And soon you fell fast asleep too.